Located in a strange ... the once-peaceful island of Gorm is in danger from an evil new threat — the ferocious Volcano Gormiti. Led by Magmion, they will stop at nothing to take over the island and capture the Gormiti from the peaceful nations of Gorm — Sea, Air, Earth and Forest.

Nick, Toby, Lucas and Jessica — four ordinary schoolkids — are Gorm's only hope. Recruited by Razzle, their talking lizard guide, they head to Gorm whenever trouble calls. Because if they don't stop Magmion and the Volcano Gormiti from conquering Gorm, its cosmic connection to Earth will cause both worlds to fall!

# LET'S GO!

# MEET THE CHARACTERS

**Nick, the Lord of Earth**

Brainy and a bit of a know-it-all

**Toby, the Lord of Sea**

He loves pulling pranks on his friends

**Lucas, the Lord of Forest**

Easy-going, he always roots for the underdog

**Jessica, the Lord of Air**

Her favourite hobbies are judo and shopping

## Razzle

A talking lizard who knows
all about Gorm

## Gina

She's Jessica's best friend, and
has a crush on Lucas

## Cannon Trunk

A Forest Gormiti who can shoot
rocks out of his tree-trunk head

## Lavor the Powerful

A vain Volcano Gormiti who can
shoot red-hot rocks

## Tormentor the Torturer

A Forest Gormiti with sharp
spikes on his armoured shell

## Ike Pinkney

The biggest bully at Venture Falls
Junior High School

## Mr Tripp

Nick and Toby's dad, who likes
to bake on Tuesdays

## Bombos

A Volcano Gormiti whose three
mouths can spit fire

## Mimic

A kind Forest Gormiti with the
power of camouflage

## Lavion, the Lord of Lava

This leader of the Volcano Gormiti
has a claw hand and a huge ego

# EGMONT

*We bring stories to life*

First published in Great Britain 2011
by Egmont UK Limited
239 Kensington High Street
London W8 6SA

Gormiti Series and Images from the Series: © 2011
Giochi Preziosi S.p.A and Marathon and all related logos,
names and distinctive likenesses are the exclusive
property of GIOCHI PREZIOSI and MARATHON.
Inspired by Leandro Consumi's original work "Gormiti"
Text © 2011 Egmont UK Limited
All rights reserved.

ISBN 978 1 4052 5684 1
1 3 5 7 9 10 8 6 4 2

Adapted by Barry Hutchison

Printed and bound in Great Britain by the CPI Group

**FSC**
**Mixed Sources**
Product group from well-managed
forests and other controlled sources
Cert no. TT-COC-002332
www.fsc.org
© 1996 Forest Stewardship Council

Egmont is passionate about helping to preserve the world's remaining ancient forests.
We only use paper from legal and sustainable forest sources.

This book is made from paper certified by the Forestry Stewardship Council (FSC),
an organisation dedicated to promoting responsible management of forest resources.
For more information on the FSC, please visit www.fsc.org. To learn more about
Egmont's sustainable paper policy, please visit www.egmont.co.uk/ethical

# GORMITI
### *The Lords of Nature Return!*

# The Fog and Going Green

# CAN'T GET ENOUGH GORMITI ACTION?

Now available:

Beastly and Keeper Kept

Coming in June 2011:

The Lords of Fate and Shock to the System

The Root of Evil and Black Salt Diamonds

# The Fog

# CONTENTS

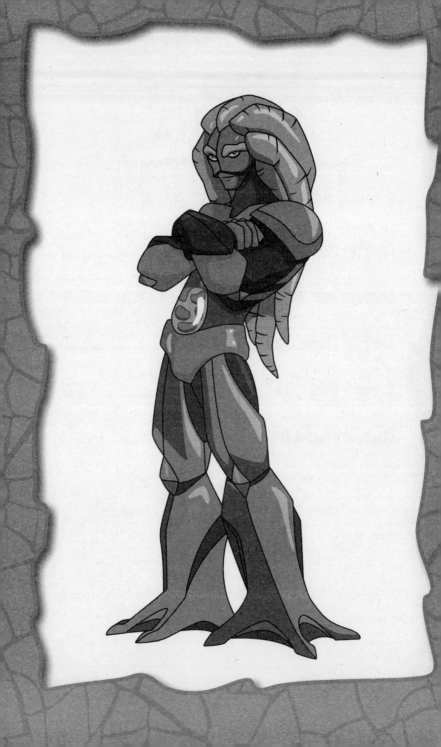

# CHAPTER ONE

# MASCOT IN THE MIST

In the boys' bathroom at Venture Falls Junior High School, a young boy turned the handle of the tap and began washing his hands in the sink. He smeared liquid soap over his palms and fingers, and squidged the bubbles together beneath the running water, the way his mum always nagged him to do.

When he was satisfied his hands were clean, the boy turned off the tap, grabbed a few paper towels from the dispenser, and headed out into the school hallway.

In the empty bathroom, a faint hiss broke the silence. A curl of white mist snaked from the same tap the boy had been using. In moments, the mist had flooded the room, and soon it began to creep beneath the bathroom door.

It was the end of lunchtime, and the hallway was jammed with people, all rushing to get to class. Few of them noticed the fog swirling around their feet. Those that did, ignored it. They'd be in trouble if they were late for class, and no teacher would accept 'I saw some fog' as a valid excuse.

A red-haired girl paused by the water fountain. A quick drink wouldn't hold her up long, she thought. She'd still make it to class on time.

But when she turned on the fountain, no water

came out. The tap gave a sharp hiss, like the lid opening on a fizzy drink bottle, and a puff of white mist hit her in the face.

The pupil stepped back, alarmed, as the mist swirled out of the fountain and formed billowing clouds around her. Before she even realised it was happening, the girl was lost in a thick fog.

Frightened, she turned and stumbled towards where she remembered the door to be. As she ran, she was bumped and jostled by other children, who were all heading for the exit as fast as they could.

When the girl finally found the door she pushed her way out, pleased to be out of the cloud of mist. But her relief was short-lived. As she staggered through the door she realised that the fog hadn't just taken over the hallway. The entire school, from the car park to the sports field, had been completely swallowed by the silent mist.

By late afternoon, the fog had become even thicker. Despite this, the afternoon's scheduled football match had gone ahead as planned. The Venture Falls team – the Warriors – were playing a visiting school. A handful of spectators stood around the field, squinting through the mist as they tried to follow the action on the pitch.

Through the fog, a hulking figure slowly lumbered towards the crowd. It wobbled awkwardly as it walked, flapping its bulky arms up and down with every step it took. In one hand, it clutched a long cutlass. On its head, two large horns curved up towards the sky.

'Go, go, go team!' cried a muffled voice from inside the costume. The figure drew closer to the spectators, and they were able to make out the football team's mascot. He was part Viking, part pirate, with a bit of barbarian thrown in for good measure. His big, rubbery arms boinged up and down, as he encouraged the audience to cheer.

And then, just as the mascot was winning over the crowd, the final whistle blew. The Warriors coach leapt to his feet and punched the air in triumph. 'We won again!' he cried, delighted and amazed at the same time. 'I don't believe it!'

As the spectators and the team stumbled away through the fog, the mascot reached up and pulled off its head. Jessica's face was red and sweaty. Her normally perfectly styled hair was damp and stuck to her head.

'Man, it is *hot* in there,' she grumbled as her best friend, Gina, came over. 'I can barely see in this thing, let alone move.' She put the mascot's head down on the ground.

'Looking good, Jess!' said Gina.

'Sounding good, Gina,' Jessica replied. 'How are the tonsils?'

'Out and gone! Thanks for taking over my mascot duties while I recovered. You did great!'

'I did OK,' said Jessica, shrugging. She picked up the mascot head and handed it to Gina. 'But now that you're better, you get to be the one to cheer our team on to many, many victories. Go Warriors!'

'Oh, I can't wait to get back into action,' gushed Gina. 'I've been working on some new moves.'

A figure appeared in the fog beside them. 'Whoa, what do you think you're doing?' asked the team coach, snatching the mascot head from Gina's arms.

'Gina's going back to being the team mascot again,' Jessica explained.

'Uh, I don't think so!' the coach replied. Ignoring the gasps from the girls, he continued, 'Ever since you took over as mascot, the team hasn't lost a game.'

He plunked the foam mascot head over Jessica's, covering her face. 'You're the team's good-luck charm,' he said, striding away across the field. 'You're staying the mascot, and that's final!'

Later still, Jessica was walking home, the mascot head clutched beneath one arm. Walking with her were three of her friends, Lucas, Nick, and Nick's older brother, Toby. The fog swirled around them, forcing them to walk slowly.

'It's not fair on Gina that they're forcing me to be the mascot,' Jessica said.

'Well, she'd better get used to it,' replied Nick. 'You've got another game later tonight.'

'Don't remind me,' Jessica groaned. She had been happy to help Gina out, but the truth was she hated being stuck in the mascot costume. It smelled like old socks and it totally ruined her hair. 'I can't wait until this tournament is over.'

'They should cancel the games because of this fog,' said Toby, trying to peer through the mist. 'How can the players even see the ball?'

Lucas nodded. 'There is something odd about it.'

They stopped as they reached a shop with several television sets in the window. All the screens showed the same images – people wandering blindly through the mist.

'Everyone in Venture Falls is walking on cloud nine,' announced a newsreader's voice, 'because fog is just a cloud that touches the surface of the Earth – and you're walking through it!'

The news announcer chuckled at his own joke, but neither the four watching children nor the other newsreader in the studio found it even vaguely amusing.

Nick cleared his throat. His brother, Toby, rolled his eyes. He knew that sound. It meant a lecture was coming.

'He failed to mention that fog – or ground clouds – are made up of millions of tiny droplets of water, floating in the air,' Nick explained.

'Hey!' said a shrill voice from somewhere beside them. Startled, the children squealed and jumped into the air.

'Razzle!' they cried, when they spotted the little lizard. He scampered up and stood on Nick's shoulder, watching the fog billow and swirl.

'Millions of tiny droplets?' he said. 'I'd hate to be the guy who has to count them.'

'Razzle, since you're here, I guess this strange fog has something to do with Gorm?' asked Lucas.

Up on Nick's shoulder, Razzle gave a solemn nod of his scaly green head. 'Ladies and gentlemen,' he announced. 'It's Gormiti time!'

# CHAPTER TWO

# INTO THE UNKNOWN

The children raced down the secret steps in Toby and Nick's kitchen pantry and into the Primal Pad – a control room that looked down over the land of Gorm. It was from here that the elemental orbs granted them the power to transform into their Gormiti forms, allowing them to battle any evil forces that threatened Gorm, Earth – or both!

'There's a thick fog in Gorm, too,' Razzle told them. He pointed to the screen on the crystal control console. It showed the same white mist. 'But it's far more dangerous. It's making its way across the land,

and any Gormiti that goes in ... doesn't come out.'

The children recoiled in horror.

'So, who's behind it?' asked Toby.

'I have no idea,' Razzle admitted. 'But I do know that if it isn't stopped, the entire world – Gorm and Earth – could be permanently covered in fog.'

The children knew there was no way that could be allowed to happen. Something had to be done, and they were the ones to do it!

'Elementals,' they cried, stepping up to their power orbs. Across the room, the Keeper's chair began to spin.

'Air!' called Jessica.

'Water!' yelled Toby.

'Forest!' shouted Lucas.

'Earth!' finished Nick.

'Reveal to us the Keeper,' they chanted together, 'and give to them your chair!'

'And the Keeper is … Sea!' chimed Razzle, as a blue icon appeared on the back of the chair. He sidled up to Toby. 'That's you, kid.'

'Let's get this party started,' Toby replied. He jumped into the chair. Immediately it lifted off the ground, raising him up until he was sitting directly in front of a control console. The console looked like a large computer and keyboard, but with thick crystal rods in place of keys.

Holding up his hands, Toby began to move the crystals around. They floated at his command, slotting into place with just a wave of his fingertips. As the last crystal slid into position, the Gorm Gate began to glow.

The Gorm Gate was a portal which led down to Gorm itself. Lucas, Nick and Jessica stepped up onto the stone edge, nodded to wish one another luck, then launched themselves through. Razzle hurled himself after, and all four of them plunged through the air towards the distant land below.

Frantically, Toby moved crystals around, guiding the others down to a safe landing. 'And ... touchdown,' he said, when the crystals told him his friends were back on solid ground.

Flipping open a magical, leather-bound book, Toby consulted its pages. 'OK, guys,' he said. 'Travel Tome says you should be in a totally fog-free zone in the Forest Nation.'

Nick and the others looked around. They were standing in a woodland clearing beside a large rock. Trees stretched to the sky all around them. Visibility was good, and they could see all the way to the tops of the trees. But that would soon change. A vast cloud of mist was floating silently through the forest in their direction.

'We're fog free,' Nick confirmed to his brother, 'but not for long.'

As the children watched, a strange figure charged from the woods and planted its feet in front of the oncoming fog. Its entire head and body was a hollow tree trunk, open at the top. Its arms and legs were thick vines, bright green in colour. It clutched two large boulders – just the right size to fit inside its hollow head.

'It's Cannon Trunk,' said Jessica, recognising the tough but friendly Forest Gormiti. 'What's he doing?'

Even from a distance, it was impossible not to hear Cannon Trunk's shouts. 'Vile cloud,' he boomed. 'This charade has gone far enough. Reveal yourself!'

Cannon Trunk tossed a boulder into the opening

at the top of his tree-trunk head, then bent forwards.
Gritting his teeth, the Forest Gormiti fired the rock
into the fog. The spinning stone sailed through the
air before the mist swallowed it up. Quickly, he
loaded another boulder into his cannon-head, ready
to fire again.

'It's like he sees somebody in there,' Lucas realised.
'We need to help.'

As he spoke, the fog seemed to solidify and wrap
itself around Cannon Trunk.

'Begone from these woods!' they heard the Forest
Gormiti cry, before he gave a short, strangled scream.

A second later, Cannon Trunk made no sound at all.

At the sound of the scream, the children skidded to a stop. The wall of fog was just a metre or two away from them now. If they held out their hands, they would have been able to touch it. There was no sign of their friend.

'We need to go into that fog to find out what happened to Cannon Trunk,' Lucas said.

'You can't go in there,' yelped Razzle, 'you'll get lost like everyone else!'

Nick stroked his chin, thoughtfully. An idea was occurring to him. Razzle was right. If they ran into the fog, they would get lost. It was too dangerous.

Unless ...

A few minutes later, Razzle finished tying a length of rope around the trunk of a tall tree. At the other end of the rope, Lucas, Nick and Jessica were tied in a line with Nick at the front. Half a metre away, the fog crept steadily closer.

'The rope will keep us together,' Nick said, 'and if we get lost in there, we can easily get out.'

'Hold on, Cannon Trunk!' Lucas called. Being a Forest Gormiti himself, he hated to think of his own kind in trouble. 'We're coming for you!'

With the ropes tight around their waists, Nick, Lucas and Jessica took a step into the billowing white mist. 'It can't be that bad, right?' Jessica asked.

Neither of the boys answered her. They just kept their hands on the rope and their eyes peering ahead of them. If something was in there, then all they could hope for was that they would see it, before *it* spotted *them*!

Being inside the fog was like being in another world. Not only was it impossible to see anything, but hearing was difficult, too. The mist muted all sound, so that even the crunching of their feet on the forest floor was completely silent.

A flickering shape appeared in the air before them. They were barely able to make out Toby's face, as his projected image became distorted by the damp mist.

'Guys, it's hard to get a clear signal in there,' he told them. 'Any sign of Cannon Trunk?'

'All I can see is fog, fog, fog,' Jessica replied.

'It's so thick, I can't even see where we're going,' Nick added. He looked behind to where the rope trailed off into the cloud. 'Or where we came in.'

Through the stillness of the fog, they heard a faint sound. Listening hard, they realised it was the low groan of someone injured or in pain.

'That's gotta be Cannon Trunk,' cried Lucas. Pulling on the rope, he led the others towards the source of the sound. In just a few moments, they stumbled upon Cannon Trunk. He was lying on the ground, his face contorted in pain.

Lucas knelt by the Forest Gormiti's side and checked him for injuries. 'He's unharmed,' Lucas announced seriously, 'but his energy level is completely depleted.'

The flickering image of Toby looked concerned. 'Who could have done this?' he asked.

Jessica swallowed hard and pointed into the fog. 'Ah, probably that guy!' she whimpered.

Nick looked towards where she was pointing. 'Where?'

'There!' said Jessica.

'Where?' asked Nick again. He removed his glasses and wiped them on his sleeve. 'This fog is so thick and disorienting.' He put his glasses back on. 'Oh, there,' he croaked, as he finally spotted the shadowy outline of a person approaching through the fog.

'Whoever you are, stay back or we'll be forced to fight!' Lucas warned, but the figure didn't listen. With a low, sickening laugh, it advanced towards the children.

Lucas, Nick and Jessica braced themselves. It looked as though they had a fight on their hands!

# CHAPTER THREE

# THE SHADOWY FIGURE

The figure thudded through the mist, faster and faster, getting closer with every step.

'OK, Toby, we need a little power over here,' said Jessica, anxiously.

Up in the Primal Pad, Toby moved some crystals around, concentrating intently. Behind him, the elemental orbs glowed with energy. 'I'm ready for ya,' he replied. 'It's glow time!'

Magical light swirled around the three children down in Gorm, as they began the chant that would begin an amazing transformation.

'Elemental powers flow,' they cried, 'Gormiti,
Lords of Nature, go!'

The fog was illuminated by three brilliant flashes of
light, as Jessica, Lucas and Nick transformed into
their Super Gormiti alter egos. Jessica grew wide,
bird-like wings as she became an Air Gormiti. Lucas
became green and plant-like, adopting the guise of a
Forest Gormiti. Nick's body became a carved lump of
living stone, turning him into an Earth Gormiti.

The three friends had barely finished their
transformations when a volley of red-hot lava rock
came rocketing towards them, forcing them to duck.

'OK, don't say we didn't warn you,' growled
Jessica, raising her arms. 'Fighting feathers fly!' she
cried. At her command, six feather-shaped blades
emerged from her wrists and spun through the air
towards the oncoming attacker. In moments, they
were lost in the fog.

'Come on, there's no way I missed,' she protested.

Nick gulped. 'OK,' he muttered, 'that doesn't inspire confidence.'

With a sudden swoosh, the fog itself began to move. It swished and swirled around Jessica and Lucas, becoming so solid that Nick could no longer see them.

'It feels like I'm drowning in fog!' Lucas yelped.

Jessica flailed around with her arms. 'And there's no lifeguard on duty!'

'Let them go!' roared Nick. He raised one hand above his head, then brought it down hard on the ground by his feet. A tremor shook the forest, and a large crack raced along the ground to where the shadowy figure lurked.

Before the fast-moving fracture could find its target, the figure seemed to fade into the mist. The choking fog around Lucas and Jessica eased off, until Nick was able to see them both again.

'This could be tougher than we thought,' said Lucas, as, behind them, the mysterious figure slunk from the mist and raised his hands.

# BLAAAM!

A blast of scorching lava rocks hit Jessica and Lucas, sending them crashing, face-first, to the forest floor.

'A lot tougher,' Jessica groaned.

Toby's face appeared in the fog before them. 'Jessica, Lucas, your power levels are super low,' he warned them. 'You've got to get out of there, now!'

More glowing lava rocks tore through his image, making it flicker and disappear.

'Come on guys, we need to vacate this situation,' yelled Nick, pulling his friends to their feet.

Lucas looked around them and saw nothing but fog. 'How? Where?'

'Follow the rope,' cried Jessica, catching hold of the line. She yanked it taut and pulled them all along it, as another blast of burning stone exploded somewhere close behind them.

Razzle was pleased to see Jessica and Lucas as they staggered from the mist, but his heart sank when he spotted the frayed end of the rope trailing from Lucas' back. 'Where's Nick?' the lizard asked.

'Oh no!' gasped Jessica, realising what had happened. 'One of the attacks must have severed the rope!'

'We have to go back and get him,' said Lucas.

'Not a good idea!' The floating image of Toby appeared in the air before them. 'You don't have any energy. You won't be able to do anything!'

'He's right,' Razzle said. 'And how are you even going to find him in there?'

'I'm trying to get a fix on him, but the fog is really playing havoc with the readings,' Toby told them.

Lucas and Jessica stared into the whiteness. They hated the idea of their friend being stuck out there somewhere, lost in the fog, but the others were right. No matter how much they wanted to help, they were helpless without orb energy. Until they came up with a plan, Nick was on his own.

Nick stumbled blindly through the fog, his rock-solid arms outstretched in front of him. With the rope snapped, he had no way of finding his way out, and all attempts to shout for help had been muffled by the thick mist.

Like it or not, he had to face up to the fact that he was completely and utterly lost.

From somewhere nearby, he heard a deep, throaty laugh. The fog swished around him, encircling him like a spinning tornado. It whipped and lashed against him, hammering and driving him backwards until he lost his balance and fell with a crash to the ground.

As soon as he hit the forest floor, the fog stopped attacking. It seemed to curl backwards through the cloud, making its way back to where the shadowy figure lurked.

'Who are you?' Nick demanded, clambering back to his feet.

'It is I, Lavor the Powerful!' boomed the figure. He stepped closer, and Nick could make out the familiar volcano-shaped head of one of the wickedest Volcano Gormiti in all of Gorm. 'But you may call me your master of destruction!'

Nick would have laughed, had he not been so scared. The evil Gormiti all seemed to love giving themselves dumb nicknames, but 'your master of destruction' was probably the lamest one he'd heard so far.

Still, Lavor was dangerous. Too dangerous for Nick to handle on his own. He had to stall for time somehow. Maybe if he could trick him into talking, it would buy him time. It shouldn't be difficult – Nick had learned long ago that villains like Lavor loved the sound of their own voice. If he could pretend to be impressed by Lavor, the Volcano Gormiti would tell him everything.

'It's probably easy for a genius like you, but I have to ask,' Nick began, gesturing at the fog around them, 'how are you doing it?'

'It's a plan that would even impress Magmion,'

Lavor crowed. 'Allow me to show you the ancient artefact I spent months tracking down.'

Lavor raised one of his huge, claw-shaped hands. A globe of blue energy floated just above his palm. The inside of the globe seemed to contain a swirl of white fog.

'The Shroud Portal,' he announced. 'A gateway to the Region of Darkness. It's where the fog comes from. It allows me to control the fog, and inside it, I am all-powerful!' He lowered his hand and gave Nick a harsh glare. 'Any Gormiti that gets in my way will be destroyed!'

Nick nodded. Stalling wouldn't work any more. It was time for action.

'I get the hint,' he said. 'But I'm not going down easily!'

With a roar, Nick transformed his right hand into a spinning stone drill. Driving the drill hard against the ground, he sent lumps of rock and rubble hurtling towards Lavor.

# KA-BLAMM!

Lavor's lava darts streaked towards the rubble. The explosion sent Nick stumbling backwards. He held his arms up to protect his eyes as the hot lava turned the rocks to dust.

'Fool!' bellowed the Volcano Gormiti. 'Do you really think you can defeat Lavor the Powerful with a pathetic attack like that?' He pushed forwards through the cloud of dust. 'Now, prepare to ...'

Lavor stopped, mid-sentence when he realised that Nick was nowhere to be seen. He had used the dust cloud as cover, and sneaked away into the mist.

'Run if you want!' Lavor called after him. 'But once you are inside the fog, you can't escape!'

# CHAPTER FOUR

# THE SEARCH FOR NICK

Back in the Primal Pad, Jessica and Lucas – who were back in human form – watched Toby as he worked at the crystal control panel. Razzle was perched on Toby's shoulder, his eyes fixed on the large screen directly in front of them, showing an image of the Earth slowly rotating.

'This fog is making it impossible to pinpoint Nick's location,' Toby groaned. His brow was furrowed in concentration, and his skin was wet with sweat.

Razzle pointed towards the screen. 'I don't want to be the bearer of more bad news,' he said, 'but it looks like that fog is spreading.'

Sure enough, the image on screen showed the white mist spreading slowly across the entire globe.

'You sure you don't want any help, Toby?' asked Lucas. He was worried about his friend. 'You've been going at it pretty heavy for a while now.'

Toby didn't look round, but gave a sharp shake of his head. 'I'm not stopping until I find Nick,' he said. 'It could take a while. You guys need to head back to school and cover for us.'

Jessica glanced at her watch and gave a low moan of dismay. 'I guess you're right. Anyway, I have a large and uncomfortable mascot costume to wear in a few minutes.'

Lucas hesitated, then nodded. 'As soon as you find him, call us.'

But Toby wasn't even listening. He was focused completely on the task at hand. Nick – his little brother – was lost out there somewhere, and Toby was determined to find him, if it was the last thing he did!

'Don't worry, Jessica, it's not your fault,' said Gina, smiling weakly. The fog was thicker than ever, and she could barely see the horned helmet and flowing red beard of the mascot head Jessica was holding, even though it was right in front of her. 'As long as the team is winning, that's all that counts.'

'Come on, Jessica, get your head in the game,' snapped the coach, stepping from the fog. He grabbed the mascot head and dropped it over her scowling face. 'We need to win tonight to get to the finals.'

Inside the heavy rubber outfit, Jessica gave a sigh. Of course she wanted the team to win, but forcing her into Gina's costume just wasn't fair.

Grumbling below her breath, Jessica bumbled towards the seating area and began dancing for the gathered crowd.

A few rows back from the pitch, Lucas slumped down into a seat. Glancing around to make sure he wasn't being watched, he opened a zip on his school bag. A small, lizard face peeked out.

'Thanks for bringing me to the game, Lucas,' said Razzle. 'Who's winning?'

'Sssh!' Lucas hissed. 'Watch it, or we're going to have a lot of explaining to do.'

'Sorry,' whispered Razzle, ducking out of sight.

'Lucas!'

At the sound of his name, Lucas turned to see Gina moving along the row towards him. When she reached him, she sat down as close as she could get.

'Hey, Gina,' he smiled nervously, hoping she didn't see him talking to his bag. 'Sorry you lost your mascot gig. I know how much it meant to you.'

'Really?' With a sigh, she rested her head on his shoulder. 'Oh Lucas, thanks for understanding,' she said, 'I don't know how I'm going to get over this.'

'Any news?'

Lucas looked up to see Jessica standing in front of them. She held the mascot head under her arm. From inside the bag, Razzle shook his head. They had heard nothing from Toby since leaving the Primal Pad.

'What are you doing here?' Gina demanded, suddenly looking angry. 'Haven't you caused me enough pain?'

Jessica drew back in surprise. 'Excuse me? What?'

'All I ever wanted to be was a school mascot, and you stole my dreams!' Gina cried. She was doing everything she could to make Lucas feel sorry for her, hoping he might finally ask her out on a date.

'But ... I thought you were OK with it,' said Jessica, becoming more and more puzzled.

'And I thought you were a friend, but you're nothing but a traitor!' Sobbing, Gina threw her arms around Lucas and squeezed tightly. He hugged her back awkwardly, hoping to stop her crying before she covered his shirt in snot.

With Lucas's arms wrapped around her, a sly smile spread across Gina's lips. She kept her head buried in his shoulder so neither Lucas nor Jessica would spot the grin, but she didn't realise another pair of eyes was watching her closely.

*Hmm*, thought Razzle, seeing straight through Gina's scheme. *Interesting.*

Toby frantically moved crystals around. The screen before him was fuzzy with fog, but for a moment there, he thought he saw ...

There! A hazy image of Nick appeared on the monitor. He was crouching behind a rock, hiding from something in the fog.

'Nick, it's me!' Toby yelled. 'Can you hear me? Are you OK?'

On screen, Nick remained completely still. He didn't seem to have heard his brother's shouts.

'No audio communication,' Toby muttered. He looked down at the open pages of the Travel Tome, hoping it might offer a solution. 'But it's a start.'

# PEEEEEEP!

As the final whistle blew, the coach dashed over to the sideline, where Jessica was back in full costume, dancing and jumping around.

'We won!' he cheered. 'The good-luck charm does it again!'

Skipping with excitement, the coach darted off to congratulate the players. Jessica pulled off the mascot head in time to see Gina emerge from the mist.

'Jessica, we need to talk,' Gina began.

'What, so you can yell at me some more?' Jessica snapped. 'You're just jealous that everyone wants me to be the mascot.'

'No, that's not true ...' Gina said. She felt bad about the way she had behaved earlier, and was desperate to explain.

'If I'm the good-luck charm for the team, that means you were the bad-luck charm holding them back from winning!'

Gina was shocked, as if her friend has slapped her across the face. *What a horrible thing to say,* she thought. *Well, two could play at that game.*

'Maybe our team wins because the other team gets so distracted by your lame dancing,' she growled.

Both girls glared at each other angrily. Then, when they were both sure the other wasn't about to add anything else, they turned around and stomped off in opposite directions across the pitch.

Nick dizzily pushed on through the fog, searching for something – anything – that might show him the way out. As he walked, he became filled with a creeping sense of dread.

'Wait, was I just here?' he wondered, spotting his own footprints in the mud. 'I can't get my bearings.'

Turning back the way he had come, Nick saw a large shape looming through the mist. He raised his fists, expecting to see Lavor. If anything, what did emerge was even worse.

Tormentor the Torturer was a deadly Forest
Gormiti who took great pleasure in causing pain to
enemies who got in his way. His skin was covered in
cactus-like spikes, and his wide, muscular back was
protected by a shell of solid oak.

'You must be the one that
pulled me into this fog,' the
Gormiti snarled. 'I'll have to
teach you a lesson.'

'No, you got it all wrong,'
Nick began, hoping they could
join forces against Lavor. 'I'm like you ...'

'You are nothing like me!' Tormentor screeched.
'I don't need to sneak-attack my enemies. I prefer to
see the *fear* in their eyes.'

Nick held up both hands in a gesture of peace.
'Look, I don't want to fight you.'

A cruel grin spread across Tormentor's face. 'Well,
that'll make things much easier for me!' he said as he
launched his attack!

# CHAPTER FIVE

# A TRICKY TRAP

Before Tormentor could strike, a column of swirling fog wrapped around him. 'What are you doing to me?' he bellowed.

Lavor stepped out from the mist. 'I hate it when I don't get credit for my work,' he growled. 'But soon, the whole of Gorm shall know the name Lavor the Powerful!'

With a wave of his hand, he summoned back the column of fog. Tormentor's eyes swam in their sockets for a moment. Then, with a thud, the Forest Gormiti slumped down onto the ground, unconscious. From behind a tree, Nick watched on in horror.

'There's no way I can battle Lavor in here,' he realised. 'He's got a real home court advantage.'

A flickering light appeared in the air beside him. In a few seconds, the light became a fuzzy hologram of Nick's brother.

'Toby!'

'Nick? You can hear me? I've got a lock on your location,' Toby said, 'but the fog is stopping me from bringing you back to the Primal Pad.'

'We don't have much time,' Nick whispered to the hologram. 'Lavor is behind this. He's using the Shroud Portal to –'

Suddenly, his tree was torn to splinters as a lava blast split the trunk in two. Nick ducked and ran for cover. Behind him, the hologram of his brother fizzled and vanished.

'Nick!' cried Toby, moving the crystals in a frenzy as he tried to get the signal back. Jessica, Lucas and Razzle stood nearby, watching on.

'I had him, and I lost him,' Toby groaned. 'But I'll find him again.'

Jessica, meanwhile, was caught up in her own problems. 'Can you believe that a stupid mascot costume ruined a friendship?' she complained to the others. She looked down at the floor, where the costume lay in a heap. 'I don't even want to be the mascot!'

Razzle shrugged his narrow shoulders. 'It seems to be that the only reason Gina started trouble was to get a hug from Lucas.'

Jessica paused for a moment, then slapped herself on the forehead. 'You're right! It's so obvious.'

Lucas frowned. 'What's so obvious?'

'Now I feel bad for shouting at her,' Jessica said.

'I still don't get it,' shrugged Lucas.

Toby cut in, silencing them both. 'I've found him!'

Lucas and Jessica dashed over to the Gorm Gate. A shout from Razzle stopped them before they could leap through. 'Guys, I think the fog is a weapon,' he warned. 'When it swirls around you, it drains your power.'

'That's why Lavor's attacks seem so powerful in the fog,' Jessica realised.

'We're going to need a way to counter that fog attack, or we'll never get out of there,' Lucas said.

Thinking of Gina's clever scheming, a smile spread slowly across Jessica's face. 'I have an idea.'

'Laaa-vor! Laaa-vor! Come out and play,' yelled Jessica, as she wandered through the mist. She was back in her Super Gormiti form, trying to get the villain's attention. 'Do you want to fight, or do you want to play hide and seek?'

When she got no reply, she cranked up the insults. 'This whole fog thing is the *lamest* plan I've ever seen! Only a lava loon could have come up with –'

'Enough!' roared Lavor. He stepped from the mist, his eyes locked on the shadowy figure up ahead of him. 'My plan is brilliant. You will regret insulting Lavor the Powerful!'

Waving his hand, he sent the fog swirling around the figure to drain it of energy. 'Now,' he seethed, taking aim with his lava darts. 'You will bow down before me!'

# BLAMM!

The darts streaked through the air and exploded against the figure. It toppled to the ground at once. A large foam head with a rubber beard rolled across the ground and stopped at Lavor's feet.

A frown furrowed his craggy face. 'This is rather unusual,' he muttered.

'It's called a decoy,' said Jessica, emerging from

the fog. 'We just needed to distract you until we found our friend. And now that we've got him ...'

Thrusting her hands forwards, Jessica hit Lavor with a glowing power sphere. The blow sent him hurtling backwards into the mist.

'I guess that's why your parents didn't call you "Lavor the Intelligent",' Nick laughed as he rejoined his friends.

Toby's face appeared in the fog. 'Guys, you need to destroy Lavor's Shroud Portal to get rid of the fog.'

'Great plan,' said Nick. He peered into the mist. 'Unfortunately we need to find Lavor first.'

'Leave that to me!' said Jessica. With her powers over air and wind, she summoned a mini tornado. It briefly blew away some of the fog, just long enough for Nick to spot the evil Volcano Gormiti.

Racing forwards, Nick swung with a powerful punch. It caught Lavor on the head and sent him spinning to the ground.

'The Shroud Portal!' Lavor cried, as the ball of blue energy fell from his hands and landed on the ground.

Raising his knee high, Lucas stamped down hard on the ball, cracking it open. At once, the fog began to pull back into the Shroud Portal.

'It's working!' Lucas said. 'The fog is getting sucked back in. Problem solved.'

But suddenly, the suction from the portal grew stronger. As well as the fog, branches and bushes began to be pulled inside. Lucas staggered as the suction threatened to drag him off his feet.

'This isn't good,' he muttered.

'Hang onto something!' bellowed Nick, grabbing hold of a tree trunk. 'It's sucking everything down into the Region of Darkness.'

'Really?' hissed Jessica. 'Did you figure that out all by yourself?'

'You ruined my plan!' roared Lavor, pulling himself to his feet. 'And you know how Lavor the Powerful gets revenge? By destroying everything in his –'

The tumbling head of the mascot costume thwacked him hard in the face, knocking him off his feet. The pull from the portal began dragging him backwards. Screaming, he tried to catch a trailing branch, but his hands found only air. The heroes watched grimly as he disappeared into the Region of Darkness.

With a grunt, Nick stepped away from the tree. It took all his strength to resist the Shroud Portal's pull, but he made it over to where a huge boulder lay in the grass.

His muscles straining, Nick heaved the bus-sized rock above his head. Taking aim, he lobbed it towards the glowing Shroud Portal. There was a loud thud, then silence, as the powerful suction suddenly stopped.

Lavor, with his deadly fog, was gone.

'It's over. We did it,' Nick said with wonder.

Jessica smiled. 'Was there ever any doubt?'

Toby's smiling face appeared beside them. 'And the fog has disappeared around the world. We're all clear!'

The next day, the sun shone down over Venture Falls Junior High's sports field. The fog had gone, and there wasn't a cloud in the sky.

Gina stood by the sidelines, watching the football team warm up for the final game of the tournament. She turned when she heard Jessica run up to join her. With a smile, Jessica handed over the mascot costume. It was scorched and battered, but, if anything, that was an improvement.

'This is for you,' Jessica said. 'I don't want it coming between us ever again. I'm so sorry.'

'I'm sorry, too,' said Gina. 'I shouldn't have used

you to get sympathy from Lucas.' She smiled at her best friend hopefully. 'So, are we good?'

Jessica nodded and hugged her best friend. 'Definitely!'

Just under two hours later, the final whistle blew. All around the pitch, Warriors fans screamed with frenzied delight.

'Now that was some quality cheering, Jessica!' beamed the coach, rushing over to where the mascot was dancing up and down. 'The team really fed off that energy. High-five for the best mascot ever!'

Gina giggled as she pulled off the foam head. 'Thanks, coach,' she said.

The coach paused in surprise, then smiled as he gave her a high-five.

Over in the stands, Jessica, Lucas, Toby and Nick watched on, delighted.

'Go, Gina,' cried Jessica. 'You rule!'

Lucas shook his head. Even after Jessica had explained it all to him again, he was still confused. 'I don't get it,' he said. 'She just wanted a hug?'

'You need to give up,' Toby told him. 'Boys will never understand girls.'

'Well, at least Toby won't,' added Nick, and the four friends laughed. They had done it again. They had saved the world of Gorm, and Earth, too. The danger was over.

At least, for now ...

# The Fog

The team jumps through the portal to Gorm

Razzle makes sure the team won't get lost

'It's glow time!'

Nick falls in the swirling fog

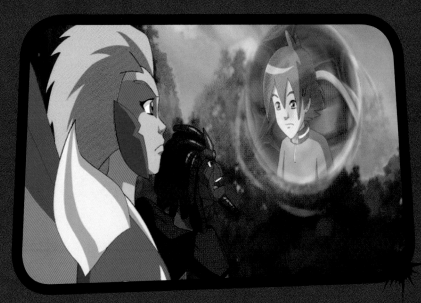

Toby brings Lucas and Jessica back to Earth

Lavor shows off the Shroud Portal

Gina needs comforting by Lucas

Nick destroys the Shroud Portal

# Going Green

Lucas blocks the shortcut

Bombos burns the forest

Lavion captures Mimic and the scroll

Nick blocks the Volcano Gormiti attack

Lucas opens the portal

Lucas goes green, and gives like a fright!

The transformation is almost complete

Nick and Toby restore the orb

# Going Green

# CONTENTS

# CHAPTER ONE

# SAVE THE SPECKLED SPARROW

In an old warehouse, standing on an even older pier, a sewer rat rummaged through a rubbish bin, scavenging for anything it could eat. Its black, beady eyes scanned the garbage, lighting up when they spotted a mouldy mound of rotting vegetables.

The rat scurried over to the tempting food, then suddenly stopped. Its nose twitched as it sniffed the air. The short grey fur along its back stood on end.

Something was wrong.

In the water beneath the pier, bubbles of gas rushed to the surface. As they popped, flickering red flames burst from within each one. More and more of the bubbles broke on the surface, and soon the flames grew high enough to reach the pier itself.

Inside the warehouse, the rat abandoned its dinner and dashed for the door as, all around it, the wooden floorboards began to burn!

It was lunchtime at Venture Falls Junior High School, and pupils were running around outside, enjoying the fresh air. Two kids laughed as they squeezed through a gap in a hedge and darted through a grassy area, trampling flowers underfoot as they ran.

Lucas, Nick and Toby were walking together just a short distance away, chatting about their latest adventure in Gorm. As Lucas saw the younger children go racing by, he shook his fist in anger.

'That's not a pathway!' he yelled after them. 'It's

a school-sanctioned nature preserve!'

Toby and Nick glanced at each other, then over at Lucas. 'It's a garden,' they said, not sure what all the fuss was about.

'It's not just a garden,' Lucas told them. 'It's the trees, the speckled sparrow. It's the purple poppy.'

'Purple puppy?' gasped Toby in amazement, looking around. 'Where?'

'Not puppy,' Lucas sighed. *Poppy.*

'The official city flower,' Nick added.

Toby raised an eyebrow. 'This is about flowers?'

'No, it's about respect for nature,' Lucas said.

'So,' said Toby, disappointed, 'no puppy?'

'No puppy,' Nick confirmed.

With a grunt of disgust, Lucas stormed off. If the other students weren't going to respect nature, Lucas decided, then he would just have to show them the error of their ways!

# BRRRRRING!

The end of day bell echoed through the hallways of the school. All around the building, classroom doors flew open. The children rushed out, heading for the shortcut across the garden that would take them to the front gate.

When they got there, they discovered the gap in the hedge had been blocked by planks of wood. Balloons floated above the planks, tied on by lengths of string. On the other side of the hedge stood Lucas, his arms folded firmly across his chest.

The pupils muttered and complained among themselves. The shortcut took almost two whole minutes off their journey time home. Why would anyone want to block it?

Ike Pinkney, the school bully who loved to push everyone around, stepped from the crowd and approached Lucas. 'How am I supposed to get home when you're blocking the shortcut?' he growled.

'Go the long way,' Lucas suggested, not backing down. 'Walking is good for your health.'

The other kids began to wander off, still complaining loudly. Ike, however, wasn't going to be put off so easily.

'Did you know this garden is home to the Venture Falls speckled sparrow?' asked Lucas.

Ike shrugged and kicked the boards away. 'Whatever,' he grunted, thumping Lucas with his shoulder as he sprinted across the grass.

Still clutching one of the boards, Lucas gave chase. He winced when he saw Ike tearing through the purple poppies. He gasped when he saw him run through a clump of trees, snapping their branches.

And then his heart sank when he spotted the nest tucked in a shallow ditch just a few metres ahead of Ike. A speckled sparrow sat in the nest, guarding her two precious eggs, completely unaware of the trainers hammering steadily towards her.

Lucas picked up his pace and took aim with the board. He had just one chance at this.

With a grunt of effort, he threw the plank of wood. It bounced once on the grass, then landed across the ditch, forming a bridge above the nest.

It was just in time, too! As the plank fell into place, Ike's foot came down on it, directly over the nest. He raced on, leaving the bird and her eggs unharmed.

Lucas staggered to a stop beside the nest and

let out a sigh of relief. As he sat down to make sure
the bird was OK, a green shape scurried up his leg,
making him cry out with fright.

'Phew! That was a close one,' said Razzle. The
lizard grinned as he took a seat on Lucas's knee. Too
startled to speak, Lucas could only nod his head.

He was still recovering from the shock of Razzle's
sudden appearance when Nick, Toby and Jessica
strolled up to join them. When he spotted Razzle,
Nick hurried forwards and held open his schoolbag,
ushering him inside.

'You've got to be careful, Razzle,' Nick told him.
'Kids here aren't used to seeing talking lizards from

another dimension.'

Razzle popped his head out of the bag. 'Yeah, about that other dimension ...' he began.

'There's trouble in Gorm?'

'Would I be here if there wasn't?'

*Good point.* Nick carefully slung his bag over his shoulder, and they all started on the walk to the Tripps' house.

'It would have to be on a Tuesday,' Toby muttered.

'Why?' asked Razzle. 'What's Tuesday?'

Nick's eyes narrowed. His face looked grave and serious. 'Baking day.'

The children gathered outside the kitchen of Nick and Toby's house. They could see the boys' dad busily mixing flour and eggs in a bowl. Just beyond him was the door to the pantry, where the secret entrance to the Primal Pad lay. As Mr Tripp would be very suspicious if the four of them walked into the tiny pantry and disappeared, they'd have to find a way to get him out of the kitchen.

Toby gave the others a wink and crept forwards. Without being seen, he snatched up a box of baking powder, just as his dad was reaching for it. Moving quickly, Toby stashed the box in a drawer before his dad turned round.

'Oh, hey, son. You've found me hip-deep in a breathtaking batch of blueberry biscuits.' Toby's dad glanced around at the worktop. 'But, uh, have you seen the baking powder?'

Toby pulled open the drawer, then immediately slammed it shut. 'Nope, none in here,' he said. 'Must have used it all up.'

Pretending to be helpful, Toby took his dad's coat from the hanger by the back door and handed it to him. Nick and the others filed into the kitchen, all smiling broadly.

'Oh, hey Dad,' said Nick. 'Off to the store?'

'I seem to be out of baking powder,' Dad explained, as Toby guided him out through the door.

The four children all waved goodbye before closing the door behind him with a slam. Now they

were free to go through to the pantry, where the
hidden stairway was waiting to take them down
to the Primal Pad – and to whatever danger awaited
them in Gorm.

# CHAPTER TWO

# DOUBLE TROUBLE

In the Primal Pad, Razzle wasted no time in showing the children why he had summoned them. The Gorm Gate, which could show anywhere on Gorm, displayed an image of vast fire that was consuming everything in its path.

'Destiny Valley is under attack by Bombos the Firepower,' Razzle told them. The picture changed to show a Volcano Gormiti shooting searing jets of flame from his mouth. 'His fire spree caused a dimensional rift with Earth and torched a warehouse in Venture Falls.'

'By the docks,' Jessica nodded. 'It was on the news today.'

Nick almost choked. '*You* watched the news?'

'I was trying to watch Celebrity Fashion Tips,' Jessica sniffed, 'but the news was all "Hello! Fire at the docks!".'

'Your mission,' interrupted Razzle, 'is to find out what Bombos is up to – and stop him!'

Without another word, the children rushed to take up their places around the Gorm Gate. They each stood next to their elemental orb and began their magic chant.

'Elementals: Earth, Water, Forest, Air,' they said

in unison. 'Reveal to us the Keeper, and give to them your chair.'

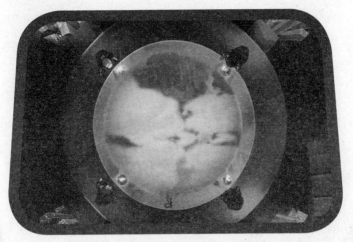

A few metres from the Gorm Gate, the Keeper's chair began to spin. When it finally settled, the sky-blue Air icon was displayed on its back.

'Jessica?' Nick moaned, as she ran over and sat on the seat. 'But I spent all Saturday studying Gormiti spell scrolls. Where was *she*?'

'Saturday special on manicures,' Jessica smiled, holding up her perfectly polished fingernails. 'The Keeper's got to have nice nails.'

As Jessica took her place at the control console, Toby, Lucas, Nick and Razzle stepped up onto the stone ledge that surrounded the Gorm Gate. One by one, they hopped off the ledge, and plunged through the gate as if it were a pool of water.

Jessica manipulated the crystals in front of her, using their magic to guide her friends down to Gorm.

'And ... touchdown,' she said, when they were safely on the ground. 'OK, guys, Travel Tome says you should be in Destiny Valley. Any sign of Bombos?'

Sure enough, Toby, Lucas and Nick were standing in the smoking remains of the once-forested valley. Razzle was perched on Nick's shoulder, cowering behind his head.

'I'm thinking yes,' whispered Toby. Up ahead, Bombos howled with laughter as the green trees and plants around him all burned to grey ash. The evil Volcano

Gormiti was so caught up in his terrible quest to burn everything that he didn't see the children. They ducked down behind a bush just a few metres away from him. From here, the heat was intense, but they were able to get a better view of their enemy.

He wasn't the largest Gormiti they had ever encountered, but he looked stronger than most. His wide, round eyes looked almost like protective goggles, designed so he could still see while he spewed flames from his mouth.

Or rather, *mouths*. He had three of them – one on his face, and two across his chest. All three fanged mouths were blasting fire at the forest around them.

'Let's power up and take him down,' Toby whispered.

The others nodded, but then Lucas spotted something strange. A patch of the forest shimmered and seemed to come alive. As he watched, it solidified into the figure of a Forest Gormiti.

'Hang on – do you see that?' he asked the others.

The Gormiti, who obviously had camouflaging powers, silently drew closer to Bombos, until ...

# SNAP!

A twig broke beneath the Forest Gormiti's foot. Bombos spun round and spotted him. 'You!' he hissed.

'Who, me?' asked the mouth on the left side of Bombos's chest.

'No, you fool!' Bombos's main mouth snarled. 'We found *him*. Mimic, the Forest Gormiti!'

With the element of surprise gone, Mimic moved to escape. But before he could get far, a large purple claw snapped around his waist, trapping him in place. Mimic kicked and thrashed as he was lifted easily into the air by a different Volcano Gormiti.

*Lavion!* Mimic gasped, his eyes widening with fear.

Lavion's tongue flicked across his pointed fangs. 'I knew if we burned enough forest, I'd smoke you out,' Lavion said. 'And Bombos here knows how to burn so well.'

Bombos lowered his head. 'Anything for you, my lord.'

Over behind the bush, Nick and Toby watched with growing concern. 'Lavion?' Nick whispered.

Toby gulped. 'He looks pretty brutal.'

'I'll check the books,' said Jessica, projecting her image from inside the Primal Pad. 'But first we need to get your powers to full glow.'

Her fingers danced across the command console. Around the Gorm Gate, the elemental orbs lit up with magical power.

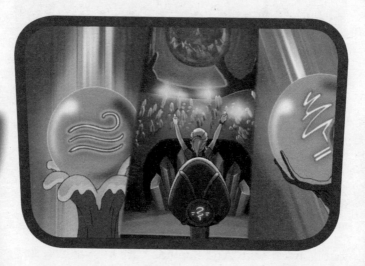

Mimic continued to struggle in Lavion's grasp. Unseen by the Volcano Gormiti, Mimic's hand slipped into a pouch on his back and pulled out a rolled-up scroll. The Forest Gormiti kept the paper behind him, trying to hold it out of sight.

'I hope you didn't forget me,' the Volcano Gormiti

sneered. 'Though it would be hard to forget such noble features. Check out this profile. Stately, eh?'

As Lavion turned his head, he caught a glimpse of the scroll in Mimic's hand and his eyes widened in recognition. 'Not this time!' he snarled, tearing the page from Mimic's fingers and hurling it to the ground in front of Bombos.

'Burn it!' he commanded.

'As you wish, lord,' Bombos replied.

'Let me torch it,' said the chest-mouth on the left.

'No, I want to!' insisted the mouth on the right.

Bombos sighed. 'Quiet! We'll all torch it.'

All three mouths grinned in agreement, then together they unleashed their deadly fire-breath.

A split-second before the flames engulfed the scroll, Toby leapt from his hiding place and snatched it up. He rolled to safety, barely avoiding being burned himself.

'Denied!' he crowed, standing upright. Nick and Lucas rushed out from behind the bush and stood beside him, ready for action. They had remained hidden long enough. Mimic was in trouble, and whatever the scroll was, the Volcano Gormiti were afraid of it. That seemed like a good reason to save it from being a pile of ash.

Lavion roared in anger. 'You dare to interfere with the will of Lavion?'

The boys nodded and shrugged. 'Yeah,' said Toby, 'that's kind of our thing.'

A shimmering magical glow passed over the three boys, and they knew that their elemental orbs had reached full power. That meant only one thing. It was Super Gormiti time!

'Elemental powers flow,' they chimed, 'Gormiti, Lords of Nature go!'

As Lavion, Bombos and Mimic watched on, three incredible transformations occurred. The children transformed, becoming larger and more powerful as they changed into their Super Gormiti forms.

'Powers of the sea!' cried Toby, as he became the Lord of Sea.

Nick's skin became as hard as rock. 'Strength of the stone!'

'Force of the forest!' concluded Lucas, changing into the Lord of Forest.

The three heroes stood side by side, ready for action. 'All right, ugly,' boomed Nick, the Lord of Earth. 'Are you going to play nicely?' He transformed his fists into solid stone sledgehammers. 'Or are you going to play with *us*?'

'Ugly?' Lavion spluttered. *'Ugly?'*

'Uh-oh,' growled Bombos. 'You shouldn't have said that ...'

Lavion's face twisted in rage. 'Clearly the hideous

pebble is jealous of my good looks,' he seethed. Then, with barely a twitch of his muscles, Lavion hurled Mimic at the heroes. Mimic crashed into Toby, sending him stumbling into Lucas and Nick. The scroll slipped from Toby's hands and rolled across the forest floor.

Before Lavion could make a grab for it, Lucas shot a length of vine from his arm and wrapped it around the scroll. He grinned and waved it around for Lavion to see.

But the Volcano Gormiti wasn't watching the scroll. He had his arms wrapped around a tree, and was using all his strength to uproot it from the ground.

Bombos stepped up to join his master. All three mouths on his body opened wide, spraying the uprooted tree with fire.

Lavion laughed as he aimed the burning end of the tree towards the heroes.

'It looks like you could use some warming up!' he cackled. He pulled back and threw the enormous torch of burning wood at the team.

'Look out!' yelled Toby, lunging to the left.

The flaming tree, with embers trailing after it like a fiery comet, rocketed through the air – on a direct collision course with Lucas!

# CHAPTER THREE

# MAGIC OVERLOAD

Nick knew he only had seconds to react. Throwing his stone body in front of Lucas, he swung both hammer-fists. They slammed into the tree, knocking it safely off course.

Bombos stepped up and raised his cannon-like right arm. A fiery stream of lava gushed out in the direction of the heroes. Toby acted fast. Using his Sea Gormiti powers to control a nearby stream, he smothered the lava with a wall of ice-cold water.

Roaring with rage, Bombos fired again, forcing Toby to summon more water to protect them. Huge clouds of steam hissed into the air as the water began to evaporate in the heat.

'Uh-oh,' Toby said, gritting his teeth in concentration. 'This one's so mad, he's steaming!'

In the Primal Pad, Jessica was hurriedly flicking through books, searching for information on their new enemy. She scanned down a long list of names. 'Lavaman? Lavator?' A name further down the page caught her eye. 'Bingo. Lavion!'

While Toby held off Bombos, Nick was doing his best to bring down Lavion. Driving his fists against the ground, he sent a large crack racing towards the Volcano Gormiti.

The earthquake sent Lavion sprawling, but his claw grasped a tree trunk and he swung himself to safety. 'I'm not just handsome, I'm agile, too!' he crowed.

Jessica's face appeared in the air near Nick. Lucas

ran up to join them. 'Looks like this Lavion guy
has been off the party circuit for a while,' she said.
'Legend says a Forest Gormiti used some sort of
scroll magic to banish him for, like, a hundred years.'

They all turned to look at Mimic. He had to
be the Forest Gormiti that the legend spoke about.
If he used magic to get rid of Lavion once before,
then maybe —

A sudden screech of fury made them whip
around. Lavion raced towards them with his claw
outstretched. It snapped hungrily as he dashed
in their direction, before turning away at the last
possible moment.

Mimic gave a short cry of fright as he realised
Lavion was coming for him.

'Now, I will have my revenge!' Lavion bellowed.

# SNAP!

The claw snapped shut just centimetres from
Mimic's head. It sprung open again, preparing to close

around the Forest Gormiti's neck. Just before it did,
a strong pair of stone hands wrapped around the claw,
holding it open.

'What an honour it must be to fight against
Lavion's mighty claw,' Lavion growled, as he and Nick
began to wrestle.

'Oh, sure, it's the one thing I'll miss the most when
Mimic banishes you again.'

Mimic shrank back and shook his head quickly.
'I-I thought I could, but I can't,' he whispered, his
voice cracking. 'I can't suffer through that again.'

'What?' gasped Nick. 'Mimic!' But it was no use.

The Forest Gormiti had already faded out of sight among the trees, leaving Nick to battle with Lavion.

Although Nick was strong, the Volcano Gormiti was stronger. Lavion wrenched his claw towards Nick's exposed neck. He pushed with all his might, until the pincer-like tip was pressed against the hero's throat.

'You'll like my next move,' Lavion cackled. 'I call it "The Big Squeeze"!'

'Uh ... a little help?' Nick cried to his teammates.

Battling Bombos, Toby turned at the sound of his brother's voice. As he did, Bombos seized the advantage. A blast of lava hit Toby's chest, knocking him to the ground.

Nick stared down at his brother, who was writhing around in pain. His muscles burned as he tried to push Lavion away, but the Volcano Gormiti's claw would not budge.

Lucas was about to join in, but he knew he couldn't take on both Bombos and Lavion. Maybe there was another way ...

'Lucas, no! Don't do it!' Nick yelped, but Lucas

shook his head firmly.

'I'm a Forest Gormiti,' he declared. 'I can use this scroll and end this right now.'

He unrolled the magic scroll, and began to read.

*'Forest magic, trees and seeds, open a portal to suit my needs!'*

At once, an icy wind whipped up around them. Behind Lucas, the trunks of two trees bent around to form an almost perfect circle. The space between the trunks glowed a brilliant shade of blue.

'NOOOOOO!' screamed Bombos, as he was dragged, kicking and thrashing, into the circle of blue light. His cries were silenced as he vanished through the portal.

Lavion, meanwhile, was still grappling with Nick when his legs were yanked out from under him by the portal's pull. 'Not again! Not again!' he howled, scrabbling in the grass with his free hand, desperately searching for something to anchor himself.

But it was no use. His fingers slipped through the undergrowth, and he found himself hurtling through the air towards the portal. Suddenly, his claw snapped tight around Nick's arm, dragging him along for the ride.

With a loud, whip-like crack, the tentacles on Toby's head snapped out and wrapped around his brother's feet. For a moment, all three of them – Toby, Nick and Lavion – were frozen in place before Lavion's grip slipped and he tumbled into the shimmering light of the portal.

With a final blinding flash, the light went out. The wind dropped, and the forest fell silent once more.

Jessica's face appeared in the air before them. She looked worried. 'Whoa! Totally massive magic spike in your vicinity,' she said. 'What happened out there?'

Toby looked around him. Bombos and Lavion were gone. Even their fires had been extinguished when the portal closed. Everything seemed to be OK.

'Lucas just rocked the house,' Toby said, smiling.

Nick didn't share his brother's relief. Scrolls are powerful, dangerous magic. Anything could have gone wrong. 'How do you feel?' he asked, rushing to join Lucas. 'Are you all right?'

Lucas patted himself down. He still seemed to be in one piece. 'I think so,' he nodded. 'Yeah. Totally fine.'

Just a few paces away, but completely invisible among the bushes, Mimic looked on in dismay. He gave a single, sad shake of his head, then disappeared into the forest.

'By the orbs of Gorm,' chanted Lucas, Nick and Toby, as they returned through the Gorm Gate to the Primal Pad. They were back in human form, which meant Lucas was eye-to-eye with Jessica when she stepped up to meet them.

'You do *not* tap magic like that without clearing it with the Keeper first,' she scolded, crossing her arms over her chest and tapping her foot angrily on the floor.

'Relax,' Lucas said, grinning at her. 'I saved the day!'

'With a magic surge that nearly cracked the crystals over there!' Jessica replied. She pointed to the control console. Some of the crystals were scorched, and smoke rose from the desk.

'The spell worked,' said Nick, trying to calm Jessica down. 'But why do you think Mimic was so afraid to use it?'

Lucas shrugged his shoulders. 'Who knows? The important thing is that Lavion and Bombos have gone, and our worlds are safe again, right?'

Nick nodded, but eyed Lucas closely. 'Well, yeah,' he said. 'But what if something had happened to you in the process? What if –?'

Toby stepped between the boys and steered Lucas away. Nick worried too much. 'Relax,' he said. 'Our buddy Lucas is fine.'

Nick shook his head in frustration. Toby was far too chilled out. Why couldn't he take things more seriously? They didn't know if the spell would have side effects. Nick remembered Mimic's words. For all they knew, anything could have happened to Lucas.

As Nick fumed silently, unseen by anyone in the room, a tiny green leaf sprouted in Lucas's dark hair.

# CHAPTER FOUR

# BEWARE THE TREE FREAK

The following morning, the first lesson of the school day was coming to an end. The teacher had allowed the class some time to read through their workbooks, but Lucas couldn't concentrate. There was a sweet smell in the air he recognised. It smelled almost exactly like ...

Purple poppies! Lucas spotted the flowers as soon as he turned round in his seat. In the row behind, Ike was leaning back in his chair, his feet resting on his desk. The soles of both his shoes were covered in squished purple petals.

'You were tramping through the nature preserve again, weren't you?' Lucas accused.

Ike didn't bother to look up from his book. 'So what if I was?'

Before Lucas could answer, he was interrupted by the school bell. Ike snapped his book shut and made for the door. Lucas moved to follow, but Jessica held him back. She was looking at his hair, and from the worried expression on her face, she wasn't just admiring the style.

Reaching up, she plucked something from the top of his head.

'Ow! What are you doing?'

Jessica wasn't quite sure what to tell him. His head was covered in the tiny green shoots. They poked out from his hair in all directions, making him look like he'd lost a fight with a houseplant.

'Ow! Not you, too!' Lucas yelped, as Toby came up and plucked another of the shoots. Nick joined them, and the three of them exchanged worried looks.

Lucas, however, had his mind on other matters. He was looking out the window at the garden below.

Ike was pushing through the hedge and running across the grass. Once again, the speckled sparrow's nest was straight ahead, but this time it was occupied by her newly hatched babies.

Dodging past his friends, Lucas bounded out the door, skidded along the corridor, and raced down the stairs. As he ran, more and more plants sprouted in his hair. Ike laughed to himself as he deliberately stamped through a patch of purple poppies, being sure to squash down every one of the delicate flowers. He hated being told what to do, and he *especially* hated being told what to do by a goody-goody like Lucas.

And then Ike saw it. The nest. A nasty smile pulled at the corners of his mouth. Now Lucas would see what happened when you tried to boss Ike

Pinkney around!

'Oh no, you don't!' boomed Lucas, as Ike closed in on the nest. Tumbling to the ground in surprise, Ike flipped over and looked up to where the voice had come from. And up. And up.

His eyes widened in horror when he realised that a huge, plant-like monster was towering above him. He had no idea it was Lucas, transformed into his Forest Gormiti form. All he saw was a ...

'T-t-t-tree freak!' he moaned, crawling backwards though the grass. Still wailing with fear, he turned and ran back towards the school.

Lucas noticed his hands for the first time, and

realised something was very wrong. 'Ike, wait,' he called, moving to follow the boy. As he tried to lift his foot, though, he discovered it had taken root in the soft ground. Thrown off-balance, Lucas fell backwards and landed with a thud on the grass.

A moment later, three familiar faces appeared above him. Jessica, Nick and Toby gazed down at him.

'Dude! You've gone Gormiti,' Toby remarked.

Lucas scowled. 'Tell me something I don't know.'

The three children took hold of Lucas. 'We've got to get you back to the Primal Pad,' said Nick, as they all began to heave. 'Maybe Razzle can ... ooof!'

Nick clutched his shoulder. He'd almost pulled a muscle trying to lift Lucas's enormous weight. Toby

and Jessica hadn't fared much better. They were both rubbing their lower backs and groaning.

Scanning the garden, Nick searched for something they could use. There had to be something that could help get Lucas to the Primal Pad ...

# THUMP-THUMP-THUMP!

Lucas held onto the sides of a rusted wheelbarrow as Nick and Toby bounced it down the secret steps that led down to the Primal Pad. Jessica hurried ahead of them, with Razzle sitting on her shoulders.

'No wonder Mimic was too chicken to read the scroll,' the lizard said, looking back at Lucas. 'He knew there'd be some back-cast.'

Toby rolled his eyes. 'Just because a lizard can talk, it doesn't mean he makes sense.'

Razzle gave a sigh and explained as patiently as he could.

'Look, old scrolls have trouble containing their magic. When tree-top here opened the portal, some of it splashed back on him.'

'Back-cast?' said Jessica. 'So it's like when some of your hairspray gets on your hands?'

'If I ever grow hair, I'll let you know,' Razzle replied. 'The point is, some of his essence got sucked into that portal, and it threw his body out of whack.'

'I'm not just turning into my Super Gormiti form,' Lucas added. 'I keep rooting like a real tree.'

'So, if Lucas is turning into a tree,' asked Nick, 'how do we stop it?'

They bumped the wheelbarrow down the final few steps and parked it next to the Gorm Gate.

'Well, aside from a ridiculous amount of luck, you're going to need two things,' Razzle replied. 'One, that scroll.' He pointed towards the control console, where Lucas had left it. 'And two ... ?'

Razzle hopped down from Jessica's shoulder and scampered over to Lucas's elemental orb. The magic sphere glowed faintly green as Razzle picked it up.

'You're going to need this.'

A few minutes later, Toby, Nick and Lucas were back in Destiny Valley. They were standing in the same clearing where they had battled Lavion and Bombos earlier. Nick had Lucas's elemental orb tucked below one arm.

'So, my orb will absorb the missing essence inside the portal?' asked Lucas, running over the plan. His entire body was covered by a layer of bark now, and with each moment that passed, he was looking more and more tree-like.

'Look what that spell has already done to you,' Nick said, as Lucas unrolled the scroll. 'Don't be a hero, Lucas.'

'You can't read it again,' Toby pleaded. 'There's got to be another way.'

'Listen to your friends,' urged a new voice. Mimic faded into view beside them. He wore an expression of grave concern. 'I, too, became rooted like a tree after banishing Lavion over a hundred years ago.'

'I stood for decades,' he continued, 'waiting for the back-cast to wear off enough that I could finally walk again as a Gormiti.' He held up his arms. They looked frail and weak. 'I have never fully recovered. To this day, I am but a shadow of my former self.'

'If that's true, we can't risk anyone else getting back-cast,' Lucas said, firmly. 'I have to be the one, no matter the cost.'

He held up the scroll before him, then turned to Toby and Nick. 'You sure you can handle being in that portal with Lavion and Bombos?'

'If you can handle that spell, then we can handle those hotheads,' Nick replied. Lucas stared back at him, unmoving. 'Lucas? Uh ... Lucas?'

With a sound like the rapid snapping of twigs, a covering of bark spread across Lucas's face, sealing his mouth shut. For a few seconds, all that was visible through the bark was his eyes, and then they, too, were gone. The change was complete.

Lucas the Gormiti was gone. In his place, a Lucas-sized tree swayed silently in the breeze.

# CHAPTER FIVE

# THE BATTLE FOR LUCAS

Toby and Nick stared at each other, too shocked
to speak. It was Toby who eventually broke the
silence.

'Now what?' he asked, prising the scroll from the
twigs that had once been Lucas's fingers.

'I will read the accursed scroll,' said Mimic, taking
the page from Toby. 'As I should have done in the
first place.'

'You refused to read it before, so why now?'

'Your friend was brave enough to sacrifice his
life for mine,' Mimic replied. 'I am honour-bound to

return the favour.' He unfurled the scroll and began to read. *'Forest magic, trees and seeds, open a portal to suit my needs!'*

At once the wind howled around them, and the same two trees curved into a circular shape. As the circle began to glow blue, Toby prodded his younger brother on the shoulder and grinned.

'Tag. You're it!'

Springing forwards, Toby raced through the portal, leaving Nick to follow after him.

In a dark cave made of black, slime-coated stone, Lavion paced angrily back and forth. Bombos knelt beside him, either begging forgiveness or pledging his eternal loyalty. He'd forgotten which.

'It's OK for you,' Lavion spat. 'You get the honour of spending an eternity here with me. Imagine the stories you'll be able to tell. But me? I'm trapped in here with *you*. How do you think that feels?'

'Why don't we just escape, like you did last time?' Bombos suggested.

Lavion stopped pacing and leant down so his curved fangs were just centimetres from Bombos's face. 'Because last time you were the one who released me from this place, and you can't very well do that when you're trapped here *with* me!'

Bombos thought about this for a moment. 'Maybe someone else will –'

'No one else knows we're here!' Lavion screeched, grabbing a rock to throw at Bombos. 'No one is going to open a ...' His voice drifted off as a flickering blue circle appeared in the cave. '... portal?'

'Whoa, so this is what eternal banishment looks

like,' said Toby, as he leapt through the portal. Nick stumbled through behind him, dodging right to avoid crashing into his brother.

'You!' hissed Lavion, stabbing his claw in their direction.

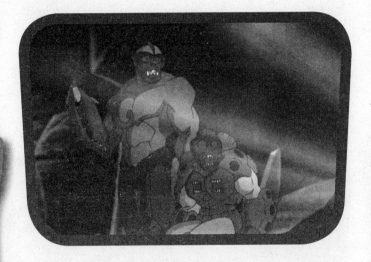

'Let's get this done before these guys try to escape,' Nick said. A magical light fluttered around them, telling them their elemental orbs were charged up and ready to glow!

In the blink of an eye they each transformed into their Super Gormiti forms. Toby's skin turned aqua blue, and his hair became flowing yellow tentacles, as he gained the power of the Sea. Nick's skin became as hard as rock, and his chiselled granite muscles granted him the strength of the Earth itself.

Even before the change was complete, Lucas's elemental orb began to glow a bright shade of green. 'It's working,' Nick gasped, as he and Toby watched tiny specks of light be drawn from the air and into the heart of the orb. Razzle had been right – the orb was pulling in Lucas's missing energy. Everything was going according to plan.

# HISSSSSS!

A jet of molten lava sprayed across Nick's back. The sheer force of the blast staggered him, and he could only fumble desperately for the orb as it slipped from his fingers and rolled across the cave floor.

Toby and Nick took cover behind a large rock, as Bombos used his cannon-arm to pump more lava at them.

'What do we have here?' sneered Lavion, stooping to retrieve the fragile orb. He held it in his claw, raising it up so Toby and Nick could see it. 'Something that would crush very easily, it seems.'

His laugh echoed around the cave. The flickering light of the lava blasts sent shadows scurrying across his face. 'It's good lighting for me, isn't it? Makes me look extra evil.'

The smile was quickly wiped from Lavion's face when two long yellow tentacles wrapped around the orb. With his free hand, Lavion batted the tentacles away, but another two snaked around his arm, pulling hard. Still attacking with his tentacles, Toby leapt from behind the rock and made a run for Lavion.

Seeing his master about to come to harm, Bombos stopped firing at the boulder where Nick was hiding, and took aim at Toby with his arm-cannon. His muscles tensed as he prepared to fire.

# WHUMPF!

Before the lava could emerge, Nick jammed a small rock into the mouth of the cannon, sealing it shut. Bombos roared with pain as the pressure from the trapped lava almost made his arm explode!

Bombos opened his mouth, preparing to breathe fire, but a fist made of solid stone slammed into the side of his head.

Toby, meanwhile, wasn't doing quite so well. Lavion had broken free from his grip, and was now hauling Toby in by the tentacles, dragging him closer and closer.

'This time, I'll escape and scorch the entire valley to a cinder,' Lavion told him. 'And in the middle of the wasteland? A giant statue of me!'

That was it. Toby had heard enough. 'It's always *me, me, me* with you, isn't it?' he shouted. He snapped back with his tentacles, pulling them free of Lavion's grip. Before the Volcano Gormiti could react, the tentacles wrapped around his face, smothering him.

Struggling for air, Lavion released the orb. It bounced once on the ground, before Nick grabbed it.

Uncoiling his tentacles, Toby crouched low, ready to pounce. Enraged, Lavion lashed out, swinging his claw down towards Toby's head. Rolling sideways, Toby avoided the blow. The whole cave shook as Lavion's deadly claw struck the ground with a crack.

'What? No! *No! NOOO!* 'wailed Lavion, realising that his claw was wedged deep into the stone floor. No matter how hard he pulled, it would not budge.

'So, Lavion, I see you've decided to stick around,' said Toby with a smile.

Nick laughed. 'Good one. Oh, and Toby,' he added, jabbing his brother on the back. 'You're it!'

And with that, Nick launched himself through the portal, and back into the land of Gorm. With a final *fzzzt*, the portal sealed shut behind them.

Magical energy radiated from the elemental orb, illuminating the Lucas-tree in glowing green light. Toby and Nick – both back in their human forms – held their breath as they waited to see if their mission had been a success.

With a creaking of wood, the bark began to clear from Lucas's face. He barely had time to flash them a smile before he, too, reverted to being a boy again.

But Lucas's transformation wasn't the only one

taking place. Yellow flecks flew from within the orb and swirled around Mimic, who hadn't left Lucas's side while the others were in the portal.

The boys watched, awestruck, as the Forest Gormiti's frail frame became larger and more powerful. Mimic looked down at his arms, now thick and strong. 'Thank you,' he whispered, and a single tear rolled down his cheek.

The next day, Lucas, Nick, Toby and Jessica stood by the gap in the hedge, eating their lunch.

'Well,' said Jessica, giving Lucas a nudge. 'Looks like you don't have to worry about the purple poppies any more.'

Lucas smiled over at Ike, who was on his hands and knees, carefully planting more poppies in the garden. His face was ash-grey, and his hands were shaking as if he were absolutely terrified.

With a sneer, Ike's younger sister, Paula, peered over the hedge at him. 'What's wrong with you?'

she demanded. 'It's like you're turning into some sort of tree freak!'

'T-T-T-TREE FREAK!' screamed Ike, and Lucas laughed as the boy turned and fled across the garden, taking care to avoid stepping on anything that he shouldn't.

For Lucas, turning into a tree had been a crazy experience, but after seeing the effect it had on Ike, maybe it hadn't been a complete waste, after all!

# GORMITI
## *The Lords* of Nature Return!

Sticker Scene Book

ISBN 978 1 4052 5389 5

£3.99

Sticker Activity Book

With over 15 stickers!

ISBN 978 1 4052 5313 0

£3.99

Meet the Heroes in 3D

Pictures Glasses Poster

ISBN 978 1 4052 5391 8

£3.99

Cool Gormiti Activity Books

# More stories and activity fun from the land of Gorm

ISBN 978 1 4052 5614 8
£3.99

ISBN 978 1 4052 5683 4
£4.99

ISBN 978 1 4052 5407 6
£4.99

Find another puzzle on the next page!

## Odd One Out

One of these pictures of Nick is different from the rest. Can you spot the odd one out?

a    b    c    d

Answer picture c is the odd one out. Nick's socks are different.

## Primal Pad

Who will be today's Keeper –
Nick, Toby, Jessica or Lucas? Using a pencil cross out all
the letters that appear in the words PRIMAL PAD.

| P | D | R | L | P | M | A | R | D | I |
|---|---|---|---|---|---|---|---|---|---|
| A | M | I | D | M | L | P | T | M | A |
| L | R | D | A | P | R | A | L | P | D |
| D | P | M | L | I | D | L | M | I | R |
| I | L | R | A | O | M | R | P | L | M |
| M | D | L | D | I | D | P | I | R | L |
| L | I | M | P | R | A | M | P | B | D |
| R | A | L | I | M | D | A | I | M | P |
| P | Y | R | A | R | I | L | R | A | I |
| D | I | M | D | P | A | R | D | L | P |

Now write the remaining letters
below to reveal the Keeper: